THE TALE OF
ADMIRAL MOUSE

Story by Bernard Stone
Pictures by Tony Ross

Holt, Rinehart and Winston · New York, New York

First published in the United States in 1982 by
Holt, Rinehart and Winston, 383 Madison Avenue,
New York, New York 10017.

Library of Congress Cataloging in Publication Data
Stone, Bernard.
The tale of Admiral Mouse.
Summary: The English mice go to war with the French
mice over cheese, but after a fierce sea battle and a
terrible storm, they all decide that cheese is better
enjoyed at peace.
[1. Mice—Fiction. 2. Cheese—Fiction. 3. War—
Fiction] I. Ross, Tony. ill. II. Title
PZ7.S87594Ta   1982   [Fic]   81-6998 AACR2
ISBN: 0-03-061221-7

First American Edition
Printed in Italy
2 4 6 8 10 9 7 5 3 1

One summer's evening, as young Tom Tiddler
strolled along the shore with his grandfather,
he saw a beautiful little ship lying on its side in
the sand.

"Can I take it home?" he asked his grandfather.

"Best not," his grandfather replied with a
smile, for he knew the ways of the sea. "It may
belong to someone. Hold it to your ear and
listen to the wind blowing through the rigging.
In the wind you will hear the ship's story."

So Tom held the ship to his ear, and this is the
famous tale it told.

One terrible day long ago, the English and the French mice decided to raid each other's cheese stores. The French mice declared that all the English cheeses from Cheddar to Stilton belonged to them. And the English mice declared that all the French cheeses from Brie to Camembert belonged to them. Official delegations were sent out to recruit mice to fight for their cheeses.

In England the sailors sadly bade good-bye to their wives and sweethearts and went to their ships that lay at anchor in the bay.

But one mouse, dainty Molly Mouse, wife of the brave Lieutenant Hercules, refused to be left behind. Disguised as a seaman, she would accompany her husband and stand by his side in the coming battle.

Aboard the ships, all was confusion. No mouse could be found to lead the fleet. No mouse could think of a plan to defeat the enemy. The great ships sat useless in the bay.

Suddenly a ship appeared on the horizon and slowly made its way alongside the other ships. Who could it be?

A great cheer went up. It was Admiral Horatio Mouse, the hero of a great many sea battles. He had come to take command. He would lead them against the enemy.

That night a great party took place on all the ships to celebrate the Admiral's arrival. The sailors danced hornpipes far into the night.

The next day, Admiral Mouse summoned the
four most important captains. One small mouse
rowed them across the choppy water to his
flagship.

Admiral Mouse outlined a brilliant plan. He would divide his fleet in two, and trap the enemy between the two halves. In his excitement, he leaped from his chair and cried:

"We'll blow the Frenchies from the seas. We'll teach them not to steal our cheese. Paris and Calais, Nice and Narbonne, They'll be sorry when their cheeses are gone."

The fleet set sail that very day, with Admiral
Mouse at the helm. After four days at sea,
Lieutenant Hercules Mouse, aboard the leading
frigate, finally spied the enemy.

Molly stood by his elbow as he signaled to
Horatio: E-N-E-M-Y L-E-A-V-I-N-G
P-O-R-T. W-I-N-D B-L-O-W-I-N-G
S-O-U-T-H-E-R-L-Y. I C-A-N S-M-E-L-L
T-H-E-I-R C-H-E-E-S-E-S.

Admiral Mouse sniffed the air. He too could smell the cheeses. Camembert, Brie, and Roquefort from France. Burgos, Manchego, and Cabrales from Spain.

He hoisted his first signal: P-R-E-P-A-R-E F-O-R B-A-T-T-L-E.

The English fleet approached the enemy lines.
It was at twelve noon that day, the twenty-first
of October, that Horatio Mouse addressed his men:

"England expects that every mouse will do
his duty, so . . .
Prepare to bring me back the Brie,
The Camembert, and the ripe Ervy.
Seize the cheese riddled with holes.
Frenchies' stores, make them your goals."

But Admiral Pierre Mouse, the French commander, who had smelled the approach of the English cheeses, had other ideas, and ordered his men:

"They shall not be allowed to pass, so . . .
Attack all the Double Gloucester,
The Blue Stilton, and Red Leicester.
Make Horatio's mice look silly.
Sink his precious Caerphilly."

Behind the French were their allies the
Spanish. They had all gotten out of bed rather
late and Admiral Santa Ana Mouse addressed
his men between loud yawns:

    "Raid the English cheeses (yawn).
    Destroy them as you pleases (yawn).
    Let no single crumb remain (yawn).
    For the glory that is Spain (yawn)."

Guns were brought out on all the ships. The biggest guns on the lower decks, the medium guns on the middle deck, and the lightest guns on the top deck.

Admiral Horatio ordered the first cannon to be fired.

The battle that followed was as fierce as any mouse could remember. First the English seemed to be winning, then the French and Spanish.

On all sides, sailors were performing deeds of great courage and gallantry.

The situation was desperate. Admiral Horatio
called every mouse on deck. Even the chef
padlocked his larder and came up, armed to the
teeth.

For one terrible moment, it even seemed that
Admiral Horatio Mouse might be lost. A
cannonball burst through the side of his ship,
and it was only the quick-thinking of a Captain
that saved him.

"Jump!" the Captain cried, and by a whisker,
they both leaped over the flying ball.

In the confusion, a bucket of water used to cool
the cannon shot was emptied over the head of
one small mouse.

Then, when the fighting was at its fiercest, a fearful shudder shook the ships. It was the beginning of a terrible storm!

All the ships tossed and rolled. The great ships were being wrecked and sailors were thrown into the sea.

There was no time for fighting.

In the water, the mice clung desperately to
pieces of timber. The dreadful battle was
forgotten, as friend and foe helped one another.
Spanish and French mice helped English mice.
English mice helped French and Spanish mice.

Brave Lieutenant Hercules found a barrel from
a Spanish ship. He and Molly rode astride it,
undaunted by the raging sea.

It seemed that there was no hope for the desperate sailors, when suddenly they saw a sail on the horizon. It was Merchant Seaman Mouse steering toward them in his sturdy vessel.

With great bravery, he and his crew lowered their boats and rescued every single mouse from the sea.

Aboard Merchant Seaman Mouse's ship, the
three Admirals were quickly shown to the best
room. They were given warm towels and
served the tastiest morsels of cheese. As they
sat with their feet in hot mustard baths, they
all began to think how much more comfortable
they were at peace than at war. Admiral
Horatio rose to speak for them all:

"Let's stop fighting on the High Seas.
To each of us his country's own cheese. Battles
are boring and tiresome and dull. We'll go
home where our cellars are full."

He raised his glass. "Atishoo!" he sneezed.
"Your good health, gentlemen." "Atishoo!
Salut!" answered Admiral Pierre. "Atishoo!
Felicidad!" echoed the Spanish Admiral. They
all drank to it.

At the water's edge, Tom Tiddler put his ear
closer to the little ship. He could just make out
the sound of glasses emptying as the wind fell
silent.